Diamond Land

Rita Williams-Garcia

SCHOLASTIC INC.

New York   Toronto   London   Auckland   Sydney
Mexico City   New Delhi   Hong Kong   Buenos Aires

Illustrations
Shawn Barber

WITHDRAWN

Property Of
Wisconsin School for the Deaf

Developed by ONO Books in cooperation with Scholastic Inc.

No part of this publication may be reproduced in whole or in part, or stored in a retrieval system, or transmitted in any form or by any means, electronic, mechanical, photocopying, recording, or otherwise, without written permission of the publisher. For information regarding permission, write to Scholastic Inc., 557 Broadway, New York, NY 10012.

Text copyright © 2003 by Rita Williams-Garcia.
Illustrations copyright © 2003 by Shawn Barber.
All rights reserved. Published by Scholastic Inc.
Printed in the U.S.A.

ISBN 0-439-57920-1

SCHOLASTIC, SCHOLASTIC ACTION, and associated logos and designs are trademarks and/or registered trademarks of Scholastic Inc.

LEXILE is a registered trademark of MetaMetrics, Inc.

5   6   7   8   9   10   23   12 11 10 09 08

3200001123656946

Contents

WITHDRAWN

Welcome to This Book

What words come to mind when you see diamonds? Beautiful? Expensive? Classy? But if you knew where they come from, you might change your mind.

A South African named Ayize did. He finds out the truth about diamonds when he looks for work in the mines. He is hoping to earn enough money to replace the cattle on his farm that got sick and died.

Ayize soon learns that the mines give up few diamonds. But they take many lives. Will Ayize find his fortune? Or will he die trying?

Target Words These words will help you understand Ayize's journey.

- **desperate:** without hope and willing to do anything to make the situation better
  Having no money can make people desperate.

- **determined:** refusing to give up
  Ayize is determined to work in the mines.

- **precious:** worth a lot, either in money or for personal reasons
  Diamonds are precious, but so are the beads that Ayize's girlfriend gives him.

Reader Tips Here's how to get the most from this book.

- **Chapter Titles** Each chapter title gives readers an idea about the events that take place in that chapter. For instance, in Chapter 1, "Blood in the Pasture," the reader first learns about Ayize's cattle. Notice the chapter titles to get a better idea of what will happen next in the story.

- **Setting** Setting is when and where a story takes place. Keep the story's time and place in mind as you read. It may help explain how the characters think and act.

1

Blood in the Pasture

**The great red bull is dead and
I, Ayize, must replace him.**

I stood on a large jagged rock and called out to my brothers. It was time to gather the cattle and bring them home. The cows had drunk their fill at the river. The Zulu sun would soon set over the hills.

My youngest brother Joseph climbed up on the rock. "Ayize," he called.

I pretended not to hear him. A little brother must wait for the older brother to speak first.

"Ah-yee-zee!" he called again. That is my name. It is Zulu for "it will come."

I grunted at him.

"How big is our homeland?" he asked me.

I told him, "as far as your eyes can see." I felt wise—like our father.

"As far as those trees?" he asked.

"Much farther," I said.

"As far as those hills?" He stretched his arm.

"Much, much farther," I said.

This game reminds us of the Zulu people. It reminds us that Zulu warriors were once powerful and that Zulu land spread far and wide. Joseph loves to hear stories about the Zulu warriors.

We sat and I told him for the thousandth time about the Dutch farmer's son. He found a huge stone on this land. The stone held light and all were amazed by its rare beauty. News traveled about the stone. They called it a diamond.

Soon more Dutch, then the British, came in search of diamonds. The Zulus were mighty, but they could not defeat the world. In the end, the Zulus were pushed back into homelands much smaller than the land they once claimed.

Heads Up!

The Zulus lived in South Africa long before the Europeans arrived. Why did the Europeans want to take the Zulus' land?

"Ayize! Ah-yee-zee! Come! Come!"

It was our brother Tuli, running up the hill.

"Tuli! What is it?" I asked.

Tuli was out of breath. "The red bull! He won't come!"

"Stay here!" I told Joseph.

I jumped off of the rock. Tuli and I ran toward the river where the cattle drank.

The cows wandered in the **pasture.** Their moans were loud and strange.

The red bull was down on his belly. Coka lashed at the bull with a tree branch. The bull could only moan. *Slash!* He gave the animal another hard blow.

"No!" I said, and bent down to get a better look. The bull's eyes were thick with slime. "Hold him down," I ordered my two brothers.

Tuli held the bull's neck while Coka grabbed his horns. I didn't trust the wounded animal. He was strong enough to **gore** me with his horns.

I pried open his mouth. He fought me, but I was stronger. The red bull let out a moan that came from his gut. His tongue was also black and full of slime.

"Tuli, bring Joseph home. Then get Father. Run home! Now!"

Within minutes my father came running with his rifle. "Stand away," my father ordered.

I rose to my feet and stood next to my father.

The red bull moaned in agony. He was the pride of our herd, strong and massive. He alone was worth four cows. In two years he was to be given to my beloved Zindzi's family for *labola*. *Labola* means "bride price." It is a gift to the bride's family.

My father aimed the rifle and fired two shots. The other cows panicked and began to scatter. Coka and Tuli chased after them.

"We have to check the rest of the herd," my father told me.

One by one, we forced open their mouths to see their tongues. Carefully we lifted their hooves.

My father waited until my brothers and the two cows had gone. Then he raised his rifle and shot the seven cows that were **diseased.**

"Quickly, Ayize," he said. "We must start a fire and burn the sick cows. People are hungry. They will try to eat this meat."

"We have to check the rest of the herd," Ayize's father says.

My father and I stayed behind to watch the flames die. The smell of the burning meat and hide was strong.

Cows are valuable to our family, as valuable as money. How could he just shoot them? There had to be a better way. Couldn't my grandmother, Gogo, save them with her tree bark medicine? It had worked once before.

What would we do with only two cows left? How would we feed our family? Or pay the bride price to Zindzi's family?

Questions ran through my mind, but I stayed quiet. I had to wait for my father to speak first.

Black smoke filled the air. We began our walk home.

Finally he spoke. "When I slept last night, there were two bulls and eight cows in my **kraal.** Tonight, there are only two cows in my *kraal.*"

—Heads Up!—

The cattle are important to Ayize's family because they raise them for meat and milk. The bull was especially important to Ayize. Why?

I thought Father shot our cows too quickly, but it was my fault. Shame stabbed me. Had I watched after the cows, I might have seen their sickness earlier. Then Gogo could have saved them. Instead of telling Joseph Zulu stories, I should have taught Tuli and Coka how to tend the cattle.

"Father," I said, "I'll replace the herd."

We walked in silence before he asked, "And how will you do this?"

I said, "I'll leave home for a time and work in the diamond mines."

My father said nothing more. This meant he agreed.

┌─Heads Up!─
Ayize believes it's his fault that his father had to shoot the cows. Do you agree? Why or why not?

CHAPTER

Beads From Zindzi

It is time to say good-bye and leave my home.
The mines are waiting.

News spread quickly of my plans to work in the diamond mines. Neighbors came to give advice and to say good-bye. Usually a cow is killed for a farewell. Meat is grilled for family and neighbors to enjoy. But with only two cows left in our *kraal*, there would be no barbecue.

In the distance I saw Zindzi and her brothers. I stood at once to greet them. I didn't want Zindzi to see me feeling **pity** for myself.

I greeted Zindzi's brothers first. Her twin brothers and I are the same age, 16. We attended school as boys and herded cattle together in the grasslands. But once our families had spoken about Zindzi's bride price, everything changed between us.

Now Zindzi's brothers treated me as a **suitor.** As a suitor I was never allowed to be alone with Zindzi.

Her brothers warned me about the diamond mines. Many had gone to work in the mines. They returned sick or didn't return at all.

"I'll be all right in the mines," I told them.

Then they gave Zindzi and me a moment to say our good-byes.

Zindzi didn't seem sad to see me go. Instead, she was **radiant.** Her smile and eyes shimmered like sun specks on water.

I said, "When I return there will be feasting."

Zindzi laughed at my boast. "When you *leave*, there will be feasting."

Zindzi was unlike any girl I knew. She was clever and beautiful. I only finished my one-to-seven schooling to see her in class each day.

─Heads Up!─

Look up suitor *in the glossary. Why do you think Ayize and Zindzi are never allowed to be alone once he becomes her suitor?*

"There will be weeping when I walk over those hills," I said.

"You're right, Ayize," she said. "I'll comfort your mother and Gogo when they cry."

Zindzi's face remained brave and carefree. I knew she'd miss me. She walked a distance to say good-bye.

"I'll return before planting season is over. I'll bring two red bulls stronger than the one I lost."

"Planting season!" she mocked. "When you return with two red bulls, I'll be a grandmother. I'll tell my children's children, 'Look! There is my childhood friend, Ayize. He is an old man with two red bulls and no bride.'"

"Don't worry, Zindzi. I'll earn the bride price soon," I told her.

Zindzi's brothers were growing tired of our long good-byes. Quickly, Zindzi took a string of white beads from her belt. I was glad to see their white coloring. Her white beads said, "My thoughts stay with you."

There was never any doubt of Zindzi's true feelings. I was **determined** to find the diamond mines and earn the bride price before too long.

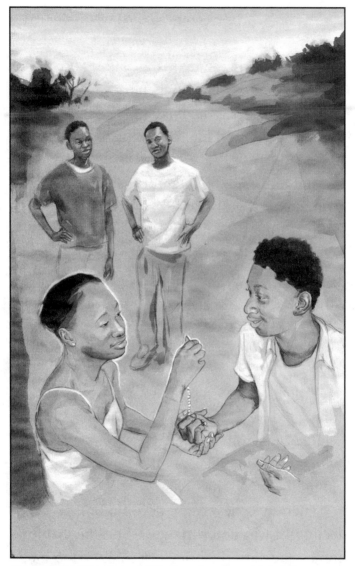

Zindzi's white beads say, "My thoughts stay with you."

A Warning

Father Thomas says the mines are dangerous.
But what does he really know?

"Go to the school before you set out for the mines," my father advised. "You must learn more before you leave the homeland." Then he gave me two hundred **rand.**

I slipped my knife in my belt and put the money in my pants pocket. I took the sack of food and drink that my mother gave me and left the hut.

The sun was still rising. My brothers drove the two cows out to the pasture.

"Ayize! Ah-yee-zee!"

I heard Joseph call but I wouldn't look back. The next time I see our hut I'll be driving ten cows into our *kraal.*

The school wasn't far—only three **kilometers** from my home. There I learned to read and speak English and **Afrikaans.** It was math that I enjoyed. I figured that once I learned to count *rand,* I couldn't be cheated.

Father Thomas, the priest, waved to me. He was once my teacher.

"Look at you, Ayize. You're practically a man."

I stood taller than the priest. I was insulted that he saw a child in me.

"To what do I owe this visit? Have you changed your mind about being baptized?"

Most of the students who attended the school were baptized as Christians. But Gogo wouldn't hear of it.

"No, Father Thomas. I've come for advice."

We went inside the school. "How can I help you?" he asked, pleased that I sought him out.

"I have to find work in the diamond mines," I told him.

The look of pleasure in his face fell flat. It was replaced by concern and disappointment.

"That work is dangerous and unwise for a boy with your education," the priest said.

I had seven years of school, which was more schooling than most had.

"You're intelligent, Ayize. You can read. You don't have to work in the diamond mines."

"I've lost our cattle," I said. "All but two. My family will starve without cattle. And I have to pay Zindzi's family the bride price."

Father Thomas didn't take me seriously. "Ayize, your mother and grandmother can feed the village from their garden. Your family will never starve. And, you're too young to marry."

Why did my father send me to the priest? Father Thomas didn't understand.

"With work in the mines, I could earn enough *rand* quickly," I said.

The man's face twisted. "My son, many go in search of glittering diamonds, but they don't find them. Instead, they lose their way home."

"I don't care for diamonds," I said. "I care only for the money I can earn for cattle. Father Thomas, I can earn a fortune."

Again, Father Thomas shook his head. "My son, you will see. Blacks don't gain wealth in the diamond mines."

This was strange talk from Father Thomas. He taught us there was no black or white in God's eyes.

"Ayize, let me find you work in the factories," he offered.

"No, Father," I said. "I must work in the diamond mines. It's the only way."

Father Thomas sighed heavily, then left me. He returned with a pair of dark green pants, shoes, and a thin tee shirt. "Work in the mines is dirty, hard work. You'll need one change of clothes."

I removed my sandals and put on the shoes. Sneakers. They were worn, but big enough for my feet.

"Ayize, the urban areas aren't like the homeland. Crime is everywhere. If anyone wants your money, you should not resist. People are poor and **desperate**."

─Heads Up!─

How does Ayize feel about taking advice from the priest? How would you describe his relationship with Father Thomas?

Spoken like a priest. Don't fight. Turn the other cheek. This was very Christian, but not very Zulu. I listened only because my father sent me to the priest to learn.

"**Apartheid** is almost over," the priest went on. "But this land stays separated into black and white. It's important that you find shelter at night. Police will put you in jail for very little reason."

He folded a piece of paper. "This says you have passed your one-to-seven education. It will be useful if you change your mind about the factories."

I put the paper in my sack. I wouldn't change my mind.

"Be careful, Ayize. Some diamond camps are better than others, but none are good.

"There are **squatter camps** along the coast and rivers. They don't follow laws. They use small children to do the dangerous work.

"There are mines in Durban that are better than squatter camps. But you'll see. These mines are dangerous. Remember, everything is black and white.

"The biggest mines are in Kimberly. You can't walk the distance. You must take a train. In Kimberly they'll pay more *rand*. You might have a chance there."

I did what my father asked. I listened to what my old teacher had to say, but I plotted as I listened. Kimberly seemed too far, and I needed money right away. I would take my chances in Durban.

Heads Up!

Why does Ayize choose Durban? What would you do in his place?

Apartheid: In Black and White

In the Afrikaner language the word *apartheid* means "separateness." And apartheid laws kept white people separate from nonwhites.

Apartheid was supposed to make the country more peaceful by separating the races. But the real purpose of apartheid was to keep white people in control of South Africa.

Whites were only about 25 percent of the population. But they controlled 75 percent of the country's wealth and 87 percent of its land.

Asians, Indians, and people of mixed race were classified as **colored.** Colored people had limited rights, but blacks had none. They couldn't even vote.

Black people were forced to live in homelands. If they wanted to travel outside their homelands they had to carry passbooks. These had their names, fingerprints, and photos inside. Blacks found outside of their homeland without a passbook were thrown in jail.

Life in the homelands was difficult. Jobs were few. So were doctors and teachers. And anyone who spoke out against the system was punished.

On the Road

There are dangers out here and I must make sure I'm prepared.

I walked from the grassland into the woodland. Zulu soil was rich from rain and sun. Wild fig trees were everywhere and I ate figs as I walked. I wanted to save my mother's food for my supper.

In a while I came upon a rotting **carcass** of a kudu. With its brown skin and long horns, it looked very much like a bull. It hadn't died from disease, but was hunted and killed by another animal. White rhinos, lions, and warthogs were as plentiful as fig trees. Why didn't my father give me one of his rifles? I had only a knife for protection. The best I could do was trek swiftly through the woodland.

Then I heard a noise. It was a low growl. If I turned suddenly I might surprise a wild beast. Slowly, I grabbed my knife handle.

The growl turned out to be a rumbling truck. I felt foolish, but breathed easier.

The truck stopped near me. A white man stuck his head out of the window. "Where are you headed?"

He could be the police. I couldn't speak up.

"Do you go far?" he asked in Zulu.

I said, "I'm going to Durban."

"Hop in," he said.

The sign on the side of the truck said "Fritz the Furniture Maker." The truck was loaded with wood from fig trees. I went to the back to climb inside.

Fritz called out, "Hey! Lad!"

What did I do? I thought.

─Heads Up!──────────

What kind of land has Ayize grown up on? He's going to the city. What did Father Thomas say about the differences between city life and village life?

"Why pay whites good money when blacks work for free?"
Fritz asks Ayize.

"Up front!" he called to me. "Ride up front!"

I didn't expect a white man would ask me to ride with him. I went around to the rider's side.

"Be quick, lad," he said.

I opened the door and climbed up. The seat leather was hot, but I didn't complain.

Fritz was the size of two men. His face was covered in black hair. Besides the priest, I didn't have much contact with whites. It was my father who bought cattle from the white Afrikaners.

"To Durban, you're going?" the large man asked. "Working in the factories, are you? There are many factories in Durban."

"No factories," I said. "I'm going to work in the diamond mines."

He whistled hot air.

"You look old enough," he said. "But it's risky in the mines. And hard to find a decent camp. Whites want to work, but the blacks take the jobs. Why pay whites good money when blacks work for free?"

He made no sense to me. "I won't work for free," I said.

A smile curled his lips.

We drove along in his truck. As we climbed a steep hill, Fritz stopped the truck.

"Lad," he said. "Look down there."

He pointed down at the coast. I leaned to get a good look. There seemed to be a camp down at the shore. Soldiers with rifles guarded holes by the beach. I saw children much younger than I, digging by the rocks. As I stared at a hole, a boy rose out of it! A tube was attached to his mouth, and a rope was tied around his neck. He emptied his bucket into a larger bucket, gulped some air, and dove back into the hole. A little girl sprang up from another hole!

A soldier looked up at the road and saw us. He pointed his rifle in our direction.

Fritz grabbed the gears on the truck and pumped the gas with his large foot. The truck **lurched** forward.

---**Heads Up!**---

Fritz and Ayize stopped to look at a squatter camp. Why did the soldier threaten them when he saw them watching the squatter camp?

Fritz let out a laugh as we followed the bumpy dirt road.

"Those were squatters, lad, diving and digging for diamonds. Do you care to join up with them?"

I did not want to show any fear. I shook my head no. "My chances are better in Durban."

Fritz laughed and talked while he drove.

We drove for many hours. Before sunset, we came to a place that Fritz called **Shantytown.** He stopped the truck and turned to me.

"This is where you want to be," he said.

I picked up my sack. I began to thank him but he stopped me.

He said, "How much *rand* do you have?"

I knew better than to tell him. Instead I asked, "How much *rand* for the ride?"

Suddenly the large man's face changed. His easy smile vanished. "One hundred *rand*," he demanded.

One hundred *rand* was half of my money!

Would he get the police? I didn't want trouble, so I gave him one hundred *rand* and climbed out of the truck.

Property Of
Wisconsin School for the Deaf

Once again, I was ashamed. I let my shield down, instead of being ready. I didn't feel like the son of warriors. I felt foolish and unprotected. From this point, I would be ready.

Heads Up!

Are you surprised by what happened? Would you have acted any differently than Ayize? Would you have been as trusting?

Shantytown

Is this place full of dreamers?

In the distance, Shantytown shimmered the way I imagined diamonds would shimmer. As I drew near, I saw things more clearly. The shacks were made of wood with sheet metal for roofs. They sat side by side and on top of each other.

Cattle lived better in *kraals*, I thought.

The ground in Shantytown was dry. I didn't see grass or vegetable gardens. Just hard, gray dirt.

Nearby, a group of people gathered at a fire. They were grilling meat. At least this smelled good and familiar to me. As I walked toward the fire a boy greeted me. He looked Zulu and seemed closer to Coka's age—14 or 15. He wore only pants and a blue cap on his head. The white letters N and Y were sewn on his cap.

"You're new here," the boy said.

I nodded.

"I'm Nkosi," he said with pride. *Nkosi* means "ruler." Almost every Zulu home has a son who is named Nkosi.

"I'm Ayize," I said. "I'm looking for work in the diamond mines."

"Are you alone?" he asked.

I hesitated, but answered, "Yes." After all, he was younger. I was older.

"I need a roommate to share costs," Nkosi said.

At least this one speaks up right away, I thought.

"I lost my roommate suddenly. That happens around here," he said. "I'll charge you only one hundred *rand*."

I wasn't eager to part with my money, but I needed shelter.

"Let me see the hut."

─Heads Up!─
Nkosi asks for one hundred rand *for the room. Do you think this is a fair price? Do you think Ayize will pay it?*

We walked to a small shack with a tin roof. Nkosi took a key from his neck and unlocked the padlock. There was a blanket for his bed and two bricks for a table. On that table sat a spool of thread and an oil lamp. The floor was the same gray dirt as outside.

"Not bad," he said.

"Fifty *rand*," I said.

We agreed on the fifty *rand*.

We returned to the barbecue and ate the rough chicken. I shared the drink my mother packed. While we ate, Nkosi caught me staring at his cap.

"It fell off of the white miners' truck one morning," he said. "Once I put it on my head, the white miner didn't want it." Nkosi laughed.

"What is this NY?" I asked.

A look of disbelief came over him. "You have not heard of the New York Yankees? America's best baseball team?"

"Ah!" I said. I knew about America and baseball from school. I don't care about either. "I prefer soccer," I said.

"I'm saving my money to go to America," Nkosi said.

I made a disbelieving sound. This boy was a big dreamer.

Nkosi didn't care. He had his big dream. "What is your money for?" he asked.

"My money is for my family. To buy cattle."

Nkosi and the others laughed. "My brother, it's hard to buy cattle. It's easier for your cows to make cows. The ranchers want too much *rand* for them."

It was true. Cattle were like diamonds. South Africa had the best of both and they were controlled by the Afrikaners and other whites. My father paid plenty of *rand* for his cattle.

Nkosi pointed to my beads.

"A girl waits for you?"

I grunted.

"No one waits for me," he said. "No family. No bride. I'm free!"

"You're alone," I told him.

Heads Up!

Do you think Ayize is glad that Zindzi is waiting for him? Explain.

"No, my brother. I'm free to go where I choose." He tugged his NY cap. "When I make my fortune, I'll go to America."

Again, I grunted.

"What do you know, Ayize? You know cows. I've seen the world. I've seen television."

Father Thomas had a television, but I didn't watch it too much. What good was it? Television didn't show movies about Zulus.

"America has the best singers and rappers," Nkosi said.

With that, Nkosi jumped to his feet. He pointed his hands as if they were guns and began shooting and chanting.

He looked funny. I laughed.

"Nkosi. What is that chanting?"

Nkosi was insulted. "I wasn't *chanting*. I was *rapping*. You know, the richest people in America are the blacks."

Even I didn't believe that.

"It's true," Nkosi said. "They play baseball and basketball. They sing and rap. Rappers and movie stars wear diamonds, Ayize. Our diamonds."

This was too crazy to imagine.

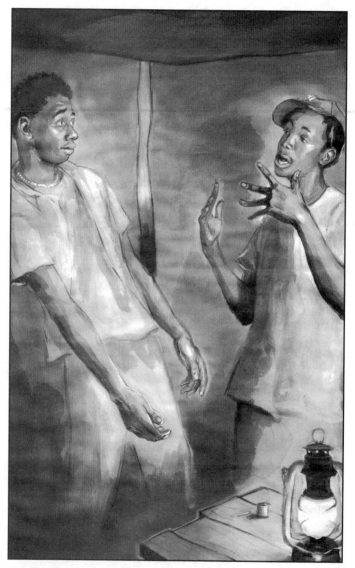

"Nkosi. What is that chanting?" Ayize asks.

"Do they own cows and land?" I asked.

Nkosi waved his hand at me. To him I was hopeless. He said we should sleep now. We had a long day of work in the mines ahead of us.

The night was filled with cries of sick and hungry children from the neighboring shacks. Nkosi didn't hear their crying. He snored like a white rhino. After a while I also fell asleep on the dirt floor.

Heads Up!

Nkosi was raised in the city. Ayize comes from the country. What does this chapter tell you about the difference between the two settings?

A Rude Awakening

Morning at the mines isn't easy. Just getting there is difficult.

Before the sun rose, I felt a rumbling in the ground beneath me. Nkosi kicked me lightly with his foot. "Get up."

He removed his beloved cap from his head. He kissed it, then rolled it up in his blanket.

"Remove your beads," he told me.

I didn't want to take them off. But, if Nkosi could remove his **precious** cap, I could remove Zindzi's beads.

"They're safer here," he said. "Trust me."

He locked the door when we left.

"New black workers make five hundred _rand_ a month," Nkosi said. "Coloreds make one, maybe two thousand _rand_."

"I need to make one thousand _rand_," I said.

Nkosi laughed as though I made a joke. "Don't spend too much money, Ayize," Nkosi warned. "I've bought only four things: the padlock, the lamp, a needle, and thread."

A needle and thread? It was too early in the morning to understand Nkosi.

I followed him to the gravel road. Soon we were joined by a hundred black men and a few boys. Some of these boys were the ages of Tuli and Coka, while a few were as young as Joseph.

As we walked down the road, trucks rushed by us, carrying white men.

We walked for almost five kilometers, until we found two trucks with long flat beds waiting for us.

"Run!" Nkosi shouted.

Without warning, the crowd ran, pushing and shoving. Everyone fought hard to find room on the trucks. Those who didn't find room were left on the road. They'd have to walk back to Shantytown.

We rode crushed together, with some men standing on the outside, hanging onto the rails. I could barely breathe with so much dust.

Everyone was coughing and wiping their noses. The ride was miserable and long.

When we arrived at the camp, the whites had already begun to work. They drove the tractors and ran the heavy machines.

Suddenly, a loud noise broke the sky, louder than my father's rifle. I jumped.

Nkosi laughed. "It's dynamite," he said. "Only the white workers are allowed to set off dynamite in the tunnels. They get paid plenty of *rand* to do that."

Nkosi and I stood on a long line with black workers. Each worker said his name, and each time the boss made a mark in his book.

When it was my turn to speak, Nkosi cut in. "This is my brother, boss."

The white man looked doubtful. "I thought you had no family."

"Boss. Do you know what Ayize means in Zulu? 'It will come,'" Nkosi said. "My brother has come! This is Ayize."

The white man looked at me with narrow eyes. Then he glanced at Nkosi. Finally, he gave me a number.

"Don't bring anything into the camp. No food. No tools. Nothing. If you want to buy food or drink, we take it from your pay. You leave how you come — with nothing. If you take as much as a pebble in your shoe, I'll cut off your toes."

I nodded that I understood.

Nkosi and I moved to another long line of black workers. We had to be searched before going into the work area.

Heads Up!

List three ways white and black workers are treated differently at the mines.

The Pit

How could such beautiful stones come from such an ugly hole?

I entered the mine and expected to see a diamond land, a place as bright and dazzling as the Zulu sun. Instead, there was a giant pit. It was as if a thief had stolen a chunk of the earth and left barren ridges with wooden tracks on them. The land was dry and gray, like Shantytown. I thought, how could rich stones come from a poor, dry land?

Clouds of dust hung over the pit, and a sour odor filled the air. I needed clean air, but there wasn't any. My throat closed and I began to choke and cough.

Nkosi slapped my back hard.

"Soon, you won't notice the smell," he said. He tilted his head to avoid pointing. He wanted me to see the huge metal drums. "You smell the chemicals. They use plenty in the mines. Then they dump the rest." Nkosi glanced about quickly. He whispered, "Ayize, don't drink from any nearby streams."

It was funny the way Nkosi spoke. As the oldest brother at home, I explained everything to Coka, Tuli, and Joseph. Nkosi was younger than me, but in the mines, he was like the older brother. He explained how everything worked.

The black workers gathered in one area. We sat cramped, as we had on the truck. We waited for the white workers to finish their jobs. The white workers set everything up first, Nkosi said. They blasted the dynamite to make tunnels. Many of these tunnels are too narrow for men.

"That's why they need children," Nkosi said. "They're small enough to fit in the tightest spaces. The black men come in last to do the hard labor."

Our clothes were rags next to the clothes worn by the whites. Flashlights shone from their steel hats. Masks protected their noses and mouths from the dust. They wore gloves and heavy work boots. Their pants were made of sturdy denim.

I watched the workers with the powerful drills. Nkosi said they were searching for pipe, which is a kind of rock formation. "Some pipe is rich with diamonds. Some have no diamonds at all," he told me.

Suddenly, the booming from the dynamite blasts had stopped. A loud whistle sounded. The children were led into the tunnels, and black men scurried down into the pit.

"Stick with me," Nkosi said. "We'll dig at the pink flag. The **engineers** found pipe there. This pipe is filled with diamonds — pink diamonds."

Blue, green, and pink flags dotted the huge pit. Mounds of dirt surrounded each flag.

I followed Nkosi to the pink flag and did what he did. We did not have shovels, only our bare hands. So I scooped the dirt with my hands. Bend and scoop. Bend and scoop. I kept this pace until my cart was loaded. Then I pushed the cart along the tracks to another flag, where it was emptied into another bin. Then I came back and dug some more.

"Very important you don't mix dirt from pink with dirt from blue or green," Nkosi said to me.

Ayize and Nkosi scoop dirt with their hands.

"Why?" I asked.

"The pink stones are rare. Diamond agents will pay top price for pink."

"Ah," I said, even though it was all new to me. "And we'll earn more for digging up pink stones?"

For the first time Nkosi didn't know how to answer me. He smiled and said, "Just stick with me, brother." He sang some kind of baseball song while he worked.

---**Heads Up!**---

Why do you think Nkosi doesn't answer Ayize when Ayize asks about earning more for the pink stones?

The "Lucky" Workers

For a thousand rand, *they went into the hole*. But will they come back?

What I'd give for my mother's pumpkin stew! The best I could do was buy hot cooked potatoes for our supper.

I opened the door of our shack. Nkosi sat under the lamp, sewing his NY baseball cap. I startled him. When he jumped up, he looked like he was ready to fight me. Nkosi saw that it was only me and calmed himself.

"You should knock first," he said.

"For fifty *rand*, I can just come in," I answered.

I put the food on the brick table. Nkosi was glad to see the potatoes. He put his cap and needle aside to eat. We attacked the food that was still hot. We were both hungry.

"What were you doing?" I asked, pointing to the cap.

"Just making some repairs," Nkosi said.

"Why?" The hat seemed almost new. It didn't look like it needed repairs.

"Stop asking so many questions!" he snapped at me. If Coka or Tuli spoke to me this way . . .

A drop of blood trickled down Nkosi's chin and fell on the dirt floor.

"Your mouth is bleeding," I said.

Nkosi kept eating his potatoes. "It's nothing. I cut my tongue."

"Cut your tongue? How?"

"I miss being alone," Nkosi said. "No one to nag me with questions." He tried to make a joke of it, but I was concerned. I've seen black tongues, but not bloody tongues. He could be sick.

He seemed to read my face. He said, "Stop worrying, little brother. One day I'll tell you how I cut my tongue. But not today."

I tried to sleep that night, but my mind ran in circles.

How would I buy cows? The Afrikaners wanted two thousand *rand* for one cow. My five hundred *rand* would vanish before I held it in my hands.

Zindzi was right. It would be years before I earned the bride price. Still, I wore her white beads and tried to fall asleep.

Two weeks passed that I worked in the mines. I didn't get used to the smell and my body ached from the hard work. Still, I remembered the children who fought to climb on the work truck. They dug rock until their fingers bled. They didn't complain. How could I?

Nkosi and I sat in our area while the whites drilled rock. A colored boss stood before us. I knew coloreds from my school at home. They were part black, part white, and part Indian. Here they wore steel hats like the white workers. But their pants were rags, like ours.

┌─Heads Up!─
What makes a person colored in South Africa? How are they treated under apartheid?

49

"Who wants to earn one thousand *rand*?" the colored boss asked.

The boss' words set off a frenzy. All of the black workers leaped to their feet.

"Boss! Boss! Pick me!" we shouted. We jumped and waved to be chosen.

Maybe we'd learn to drill or to drive a tractor. Whites were paid ten thousand *rand* to work those jobs. Maybe Fritz was right. Blacks took the same jobs as whites, for less money.

I didn't care. I needed to earn one thousand *rand*, not five hundred *rand*. I jumped and shouted: "Pick me! Pick me, Boss!"

In spite of my jumping, the boss looked past me. He picked four workers and Nkosi was one of them.

Nkosi beamed. "America, here I come."

The work whistle sounded. I climbed down into the pit and found the green flag.

Heads Up!

Why do you think the bosses will pay one thousand rand for this special job?

50

A new hole had been dug near the center of the pit. I was careful not to stare too long. The boss took money from your pay if you wasted time. Still, I could see the four lucky blacks following the boss to the new hole. A rope was tied around each of the lucky workers. One by one, they vanished into the hole.

My eyes stayed on the giant hole too long. I began to load the cart with dirt. I didn't want my pay to be docked.

Suddenly I heard a terrible sound. "Aaaaiiiy!"

I jumped. It was a scream coming up from the hole. It was loud at first, then it faded away quickly. Both white and black workers gathered around the hole.

I tried to look and work at the same time. I counted three of the lucky workers coming out of the hole. Nkosi wasn't among them. My heart pounded. I ran to the hole.

"My brother! My brother!"

The colored boss said, "It was an accident. The rope broke."

"We have to get him!" I yelled.

Ayize refuses to believe that Nkosi is gone.

"He's gone," the colored boss said. "No one could survive that fall. He's gone."

"They can't just leave him there," I said. "Maybe he's all right. There are machines here. Machines that can reach down and get him." I refused to believe Nkosi could be gone.

The colored boss was annoyed. "They don't use those machines to dig up black bodies," he snapped at me. "Those machines are for digging diamonds."

Most of the workers started to leave the hole and go back to work. Meanwhile, the three workers who went down with Nkosi got ready to go back in the hole.

I just stood and stared at them. How could they go back there?

How could Nkosi be gone, just like that? Gone.

"Get back to work, you!" The colored boss shoved me back toward my cart. I wanted to scream at him, but I held my tongue. I walked back to my cart, bent down, and started to dig.

Nkosi's Gift

***The NY cap holds my brother's dreams
in its seams.***

Zulus don't cry or show fear, I used to tell Joseph. Not even if they were being tortured. Not even if attacked by a wild animal.

Still, I cried on the long walk back to Shantytown. I wouldn't ride on the work truck with the others. I'd never ride the work truck or work in the mines again.

Let them keep their five hundred *rand*. Black life in the mines is no life at all. No one even tried to find Nkosi's body. The other three men kept diving into that hole, even after Nkosi's death! And for what? One thousand *rand*? It was probably one thousand *rand* that they'd never even see.

That night I broke into our shack. I never found out where Nkosi hid the key.

I fell down on Nkosi's blanket and slept until the sun rose. I had worked hard in the mines. And now I wouldn't get paid. But I didn't care. I wasn't going back.

I gathered the sack with my belongings. I tied Zindzi's beads around my neck. I'd leave the shack as I first entered it. The blanket lay on the floor. Nkosi's oil lamp, needle, and thread sat on the brick table.

Yet I couldn't leave Nkosi's cap behind. His body was lying somewhere deep in that hole. This was the only true part of him that was left. I put the NY cap on my head and left Shantytown behind me.

I'd take Father Thomas' advice. I had my one-to-seven paper. I could still find work in a factory. I couldn't return home with less *rand* than I was given. I headed for downtown Durban.

As I walked, Nkosi's cap bothered my head. Why did he love this cap so? I didn't understand. It scratched and jabbed.

I took the cap off and looked inside. A band had been sewn around the edges. These were not machine stitches. They had been sewn by Nkosi.

"Ah!" I said. "Nkosi's needle and thread!"

I felt hard lumps inside the band.

I stood still for a long time while my mind raced. Everything became clear—as clear as diamonds. I no longer searched for a factory. Instead I looked for a diamond agent. I wouldn't ask anyone for help. I would just read the signs on my own.

In downtown Durban, I had to be careful. I didn't want to be stopped for any reason.

After a lot of walking, I found an agent. He was a thin man with a dull face.

I said in Afrikaans, "I've something to sell."

"Let me see," he said.

I removed Nkosi's cap. I undid Nkosi's stitches slowly and pushed the stones along the band. Out of the small opening they fell.

They were pink stones with some traces of blood. Nkosi's blood. He had found the pink stones the engineers couldn't find. He had been hiding them in his mouth, smuggling them out of the camp.

The diamond agent looked at me. He put the pink stones on a scale. He looked at me hard.

"Steal these stones, did you?"

"No," I said. Nkosi couldn't answer the same, but I could.

"Only one mine around here has pink stones," the diamond agent said.

I hid my fear as best as I could. He could call the police.

He looked at the stones and said, "Eight thousand *rand*."

"Only eight thousand *rand* for the pink stones?" I used his words against him. Didn't he just tell me only one mine had pink stones? Didn't Nkosi say the pink stones were rare?

"Do you know what happens to thieves?" he asked me.

─**Heads Up!**─────────────

What do you think the diamond agent will do now?

I didn't blink, but I was scared.

The diamond agent called another man over. The other man looked at the stones. He went to a room in the back. He returned with cash.

"Fifteen thousand *rand*," he said.

Quickly, I took the money and left with haste. The diamond agent could still call the police. My heart pounded as I walked. Even with this money, I couldn't relax. I told myself to be ready for anything.

I kept the faces of Zindzi, my family, and Nkosi with me. They would guide me to the homeland. I knew I had done well. Already, I began to think of the story I would tell Joseph about my journey. Still, one thought jabbed at my mind. Perhaps I had been cheated. I would never know the true value of the pink diamonds.

I put Nkosi's cap on my head. I wanted to believe Nkosi had a last laugh at the miners. Later, I would re-sew his stitches in his NY cap.

─Heads Up!─

How has Ayize changed?

58

Property Of
Wisconsin School for the Deaf

Ayize puts his friend's cap back on his head. He wants to
believe that Nkosi has had a last laugh at the miners.

Even with enough *rand* to buy cows, Zindzi and I waited to marry. I had much to learn from my father about being a man and a rancher. Ten years later I had my own *kraal*, filled with cattle.

My brothers Coka and Tuli grew up and left the homeland. They work in factories in Lesotho. Joseph wasn't satisfied with a one-to-seven education. He is a student at the University of South Africa. Joseph now writes stories of the Zulu people, past and present.

Often I remember Nkosi and his dream to see America. It saddens me that he didn't live to see the growing changes in South Africa. Shortly after Nkosi's death, apartheid ended.

South Africans elected our first black president, Nelson Mandela. As president, Nelson Mandela rewrote many of the old laws.

The diamond and gold mines have changed, but not enough. Fewer mines **employ** children.

But some still do. More companies follow safety laws. Yet, the mines remain dangerous. And traces of apartheid remain between black and white miners. As long as the world craves diamonds, these ugly holes will be dug in our land.

While I tend cattle, my thoughts jab me. I ask myself the same questions. Do people know the cost of the diamonds that they wear? Can they see the blood on the stones?

Meet the Author

Rita Williams-Garcia

Rita Williams–Garcia is a writer who lives in Queens, New York. Her writing career began as a teenager by writing short stories and keeping a journal. Ms. Williams–Garcia's novels and short stories about today's urban teens have been published for fifteen years. Her novels and short stories have won numerous awards.

Ms. Williams-Garcia is writing more stories about teens from other countries. "The more we learn about others, the more we learn about ourselves." Here's what inspired *Diamond Land*.

"I was born in April. So, my birthstone is a diamond. And I had always wanted a diamond engagement ring. But when my boyfriend proposed marriage, he did not give me a diamond ring. He said that Africans die every day mining diamonds.

"Eventually, I married someone else. He did give me a diamond ring. But when it was stolen, I didn't ask him to replace it. I remembered what my first fiancé had told me about Africans and diamonds."

Now you know the real price of diamonds, too.

Glossary

Afrikaans *(noun)* language spoken mostly by Dutch immigrants to South Africa (p. 18)

apartheid *(noun)* a policy in South Africa designed to separate blacks and whites and keep white people in power (p. 21)

carcass *(noun)* the body of a dead animal (p. 24)

colored *(adjective)* a South African term for someone of mixed race (p. 23)

desperate *(adjective)* without hope and willing to do anything to make the situation better (p. 20)

determined *(adjective)* refusing to give up (p. 15)

diseased *(adjective)* sick (p. 9)

employ *(verb)* to hire for work (p. 60)

engineer *(noun)* a person who uses science to make things that are useful to others (p. 44)

gore *(verb)* to stab with horns (p. 8)

kilometer *(noun)* a measure of distance equal to 0.6 miles (p. 18)

kraal *(noun)* Afrikaans word for corral; a place to keep cattle or horses (p. 11)

Glossary

lurch *(verb)* to move forward quickly and without warning (p. 28)

pasture *(noun)* grazing land where animals can eat grass (p. 8)

pity *(noun)* a feeling of sadness or sympathy for someone who is suffering (p. 13)

precious *(adjective)* worth a lot, either in money or for personal reasons (p. 38)

radiant *(adjective)* bright, shining (p. 14)

rand *(noun)* unit of money in South Africa (p. 17)

shantytown *(noun)* a town of roughly built huts or cabins (p. 29)

squatter camp *(noun)* a temporary town where people live on land they do not own. In South Africa, mines that don't follow laws are called squatter camps. (p. 21)

suitor *(noun)* a person who tries to win the love of another person (p. 14)